THIS IS HOW IT BEGAN

We have suffered. My mother and I. From an affliction. Our blood needs our brains. Memories compelled by cuts seal wounds. If the past you keep with you in the present disappeared with a bruise. Then you would understand.

I notice a spot. I think as it seeps that Nietzsche said he loved only what a person wrote with her own blood. Frantic. At first. I am. Swatting. Yes. I remember. How it began. I remember. Yes. At a horsefly. I was swatting. With something to prick it in my hands. I remember.

These things happen. There's been similar incidents. Now there's inflammation, a bit of wet, a severed tendon. No. Not yet. A bandage underneath a sleeve would keep Teddy from worrying. But he doesn't worry anymore. If I severed a tendon I might never remember his name.

I can never expect what I will forget.
It could not be worse.

It wasn't Nietzsche who said that what we write with blood isn't meant to be read but learned by heart. Or it was him, and this, what you're reading, is meant to be both.

Tell me, how do you know what you've forgotten?

See, for you, there's that imprint, when just the shadow that an engram once cast in your whatever-it's-called-cortex-something is enough to make you remember when you run into Jen to tell her that last week you remembered when you recited Bernadette Mayer's "You jerk you didn't call me up" when her boyfriend before her husband fucked her over and there you were in the present of your past drinking wine straight from the bag chanting together while you squatted on an unvacuumed rug: "You can either make love or die at the hands of / the Cobra Commander." This is the tracing ribbon you cling to. Something encoded in your mind provides a clue. You can cling to. When you see a picture of your fifth grade classroom (yes, that's you in the blue jumper, the plastic glasses so heavy you tipped your head, the tinted acne cream that never matched your winter tan, all of this as you lean self-consciously into the student next to you in the hopes that you'll remember wrong: that was a good year and you did get invited and she loved her present) reminds you of the way your mother smelled like salisbury steaks then. Remembering wrong is still remembering.

My mother and I. The biological work of our bodies results in damnatio memoriae. The removal from remembrance. It sounds fantastical. It is devastating.[1]

1. It is not always necessarily so. First-degree cuts. These remove a memory. But not every memory.

Jen's husband Gary is one of the few who knew. He says you'll remember that what's orange is good for your eyes no matter what. You means you. Not me. Gary will always be one of the few who knows. He thinks that facts about vegetables become permanent. He has always hoped for me.

Jen is one of the only others who knows. She says that sometimes people need to be found with intimate microscopes.

Most people need less than this to find me. Because of what's wrong I sometimes remember people in fragments of light. Because the particle of their person disappears into a wave and I can't place them. They get frustrated or if they know they gasp, ask questions without taking breaths, see me as a petri dish. They remember me. And know that I might never forget them. Or I could lose what they look like if after we first met I handled a pile of loose-leaf papers too casually and there it is. The quick superficial slice and they could be gone.

If I cut off my arm they wouldn't call Ben.

Maybe he'd make a joke. We'd laugh like donkeys through the hemorrhaging. But I've never cut off my arm.

Can you forget a sensation? Missing limbs sometimes feel shorter. You remember them the right way but they feel shorter. Pain in empty space. Even if you forget the way life thunders, that first moment of the jumped-in-puddle thrill before it seeps cold in between your toes and becomes a burden, you can't forget what it feels like to get a finger smashed in the back-seat door of a Ford Taurus. Neither can I. In the instant there is no forgetting. This is a relief. This is a relief I remember to remember no matter what.

Maybe I should call Ben?

This happens sometimes, when something's been slashed and I start to go through my list.

Things I Haven't Forgotten

How to write a cursive Zed.
Our mother. Ben. Me.
A pair of moccasins.
How she gets when she's milk drunk.
That time I slept with Teddy's friend John.
How to french braid her hair.
That salisbury steak is minced beef shaped to look like a steak.
How sometimes I sweat through my nose.
My first fiberglass cigarette.
I am not always asleep when he thinks.
A love letter to my eyebrows.
I have a daughter.

All of these are with me as it happens this time. The horsefly.

Maybe I should call Ben anyway?

I shouldn't swing at things with sharp utensils. Unhandy hands. Clumsy comes from "to be numb with cold."

Maybe I should call Ben anyway?

I shouldn't swing at things with sharp utensils. Unhandy hands. Then clumsy creates entropy. A heat death from swinging at things with sharp things.

Except Ben.

Ouch. God damned unsevered limb. Will live. Will not look lopsided. I have become rundown like the universe.

Except Ben is dead.

Teddy and I decide we should raise something together. We agree this something should be turtles. Their shell is an outgrowth of their ribs which acts as a shield. They are protected. Their short, sturdy feet keep them. They can have two-hundred-years of memory.

We watch a documentary on a turtle named Mzee and a hippo named Owen who befriend each other. We name our turtle Owen. We speak to him and we know that he will remember our voices. We decide that even if an accident happens and I forget how I feel about Owen, I will never forget he's a turtle. We laugh. Teddy tells me:

{I will be here when you forget.}

Teddy told me:

{I will help you remember how much Owen needs us.}

The phone rings. I haven't begun cleaning her crayon off the walls. The phone rings. I'm running out of black dresses but why I have them I remember. The phone rings. I know why he does this. He's so afraid I'll forget.

Bristlecone pines have memories that lives with them the 5,000 years of their life. They grow slowly, are resistant to invasion. In their rings are the memory of ancient volcanic eruptions, Sumerian city-states. Perhaps having to hold onto so much for so long explains their grotesque shape.

The phone stops ringing but it will ring again. He wants to know that I think of him. He's always wanting to know. These things: what I know is that it's not just that he wants to be thought of. It's that no one wants to be forgotten. Think of that moment before you remind someone of your name, someone you've met before, someone you've given a ride home to who is a friend of a friend and so your name should've come up in conversation, except this person seems to have forgotten it. But the thought that you could forget someone completely is false for everyone else. Even if you can't recall what she likes to be called, you remember where that freckle is above her lip. She still has that freckle. Everyone's existence is dependent on context. It is what saves us from disappearing into things microscopes are needed to find.

Again the phone is ringing again. It's unlikely I'll forget that the sound is, in fact, what it is. The sound makes a shape.

If I forget the sound I'll remember the shape. This is how the brain protects us. Involuntary trips down cognitive highways. If it was just a sound that was a sound, it could disappear too. Just like how he's afraid his name will be stored in that house that is the architecture of memory, those rooms where we're supposed to keep things so we can find them, so we know where to look. Except my house is made of dry cement and walls, and floors can so easily give way, like for instance, if I chase after a horsefly with a steak knife.

Except when I answer the phone Teddy wants to know if he's getting ripped off. If he's getting ripped off he'll be so mad he won't even feed the turtle.

Telling people things means telling them things sometimes I swear they already know. But then they have to admit that they know and actually live with it and for that you are to blame. I am to blame. How could you know? I am to blame.

He says what we've had has been ripped. To rip: to cut, tear apart. He says it is too much and that tear means tear not tear. I say it also means to subject to vehement criticism or attack. The subject being subjected to isn't Teddy. He tells me to finish my sentence. I tell him I thought it might be time he'd like to know. In our other definition of tear we might be inching closer: "to move quickly or violently" to a place one of us might not survive to see.

He's not pissed because I have revealed myself too soon, but that it should've been said before we began. But to punish the turtle, in the end, that is too much. How could anyone trust someone who would punish the turtle?

Everyone forgets. Phrasal verbs are for those foreigners who, unlucky enough to study English, will at some point feel the need to memorize 2,616 multi-word verbs they might not forget. To tear: apart, up, down, away, off, into.

It's not as if the turtle can tell the difference; if you don't feed him he knows he hasn't been fed. He won't understand that his hunger is because I didn't tell you what I am. That, I can't explain.

If Teddy's been cheated then what's been stolen? There is, of course, his time. Energy put into another: this is the entropy of a "we." The dispersal of energy, that's all it is. Maybe it was time he was less spread out than he's been.

If it hadn't happened, I might not have ever told him. I bumped my knee on a sharp edge and it happened. It's not particularly interesting to watch. I do not wear my hippocampus on my sleeve.

All of this leads up to this.

When my skin breaks a brief constriction of vessels reduces blood flow to the wound, alerts my brain it must have a memory to activate platelets to form a clot to block the bleeding vessels.

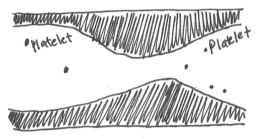

My nervous system removes one memory for each breach of epidermis. My memory removes damaged tissue. An inflammatory response. My debris reabsorbs my body,

lays down a new tissue framework. Blood flow to the wound increases. In my brain the spot once occupied by this speck of past droops empty. The process takes little time. I heal.

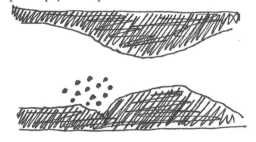

And a   mory is lost.

I have a condition. It is like ~~a fuse with a saber that waits disability~~
easier to cut a hole in ~~grey matter unhappy synapse punchdrunk~~
a wall than to break my skin so ~~past not in gait or movement but~~
it cannot heal. It is easier to cut a whole in ~~a timeline of flesh~~

Everyone who knows wonders why.

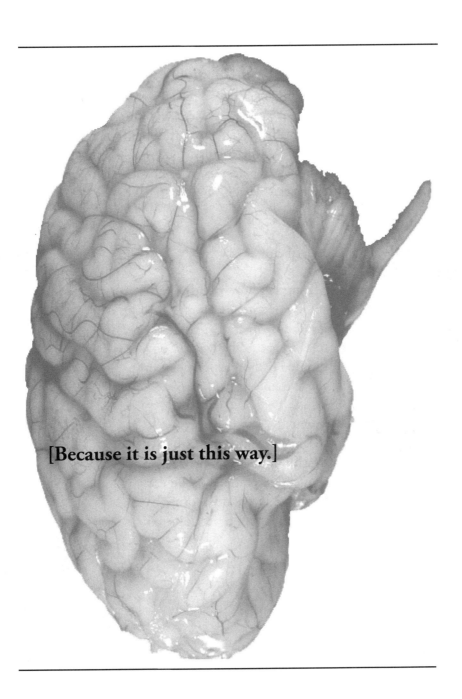

[Because it is just this way.]

My mother suffered a similar affliction. When I was born they cut her to make room for my overdue head. They pulled. She began to heal. Her skin closing over me. A nurse wouldn't hold her hand. They cut her again. Had to rip her long. Rumors of this occurrence spread. Luckily, we grew up in Richland Center, Wisconsin, Frank Lloyd Wright's hometown. There was little chance of us cementing permanent celebrity status.

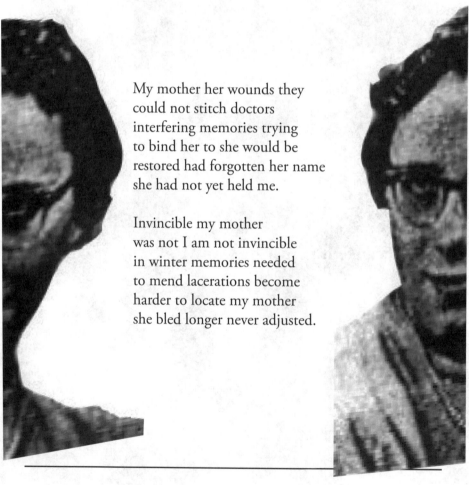

My mother her wounds they
could not stitch doctors
interfering memories trying
to bind her to she would be
restored had forgotten her name
she had not yet held me.

Invincible my mother
was not I am not invincible
in winter memories needed
to mend lacerations become
harder to locate my mother
she bled longer never adjusted.

Neither could Ben, my adopted brother.
Unafflicted, chock-full of recollections

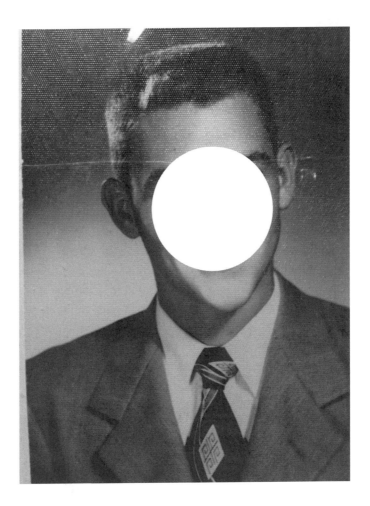

It's never *quite* right. The way people throw themselves out of windows.

How an Absence Becomes a Presence

Ben is like a phantom limb.
There is the pain.
And here am I.
See the limb on the sidewalk.
The only way to feel what's not there is if.
There's pain in it often.
At night I would try with one lost hand to grope.
For the other.
It's the image that will stem.
The flow of time gains weight.
As we get older we lose.
More limbs whose weight we cannot bear.

The way some ~~handkerchiefs are unexpectedly needed for unnamed pain.~~
Harmonies become discrepancies ~~that will be parallel and converge~~
The way what's not derived ~~from one word cannot mean its opposite~~
Becomes confounded.

After three weeks of near intimacy, of Teddy finding the dip in my achilles in the night, of thinking it enchanting, my not wanting to handle paper or open hot sauce bottles with kitchen knives, he left a note in my shoe.

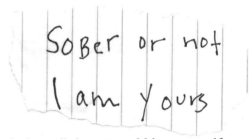

I would not push the pull door. I could keep myself secret. I would win by waiting. This afforded seclusion. Would I have won by waiting longer?

It's best when there are months between cuts. Build up the in- between. That the dream you thought you had with a beaver and Abraham Lincoln was a sleeping-pill commercial; the man on the phone in the street who asked, "Now what's this business about reincarnation?"; the old woman with flowers in her hands waiting for the bus that should've been there but wasn't while an even older woman played the trumpet for her while she waited then walking seventeen blocks to the next bus stop so as not to disrupt that perfection; the there can be no monument to democracy; the nickel warmed on the sidewalk; the way prepositions get underneath fingernails; the use of nincampoop in a sentence; the don't threaten me with a good time; the on public transportation not wanting to touch strangers' wet elbows; the wondering what kind of people get manicures; the purchase of toothpaste with a coupon; the disappointing games of Scrabble; the cigarette hangover; the heap of socks and Linux manual on Lexington & 19th street; the I'm less pretty in winter; the working-class cashmere; the that ten stitches was a lot of stitches back then; the when in Rome don't punch Romans; the powdered sugar condolences; the I don't look 55, that's the time warp; the there should never be elevators in cabins; the fake gold watch with the real gold chain; the donated by the Sara Lee Corporation; the solitary anguish of ordinary individuals; the that some poems, like bells, seem heavy until heard; the pinwheels in the breeze; the wondering who invented noodles; the I want to be a hive; the homage to the romantic bullet; the I've never been blonde or been punched; the you smell like the day before yesterday; the never having seen a bristlecone pine; the at one time the function of the beard was probably to make it easier to tell males and females apart; the new mother that smelled of cinnamon; "the grass turns yellow secretly" somewhere; the did I smell like a spice then too; the defensiveness of Midwestern cities; the that Emily Dickinson signed a letter, "my hand trembles." It is this that should clot the cuts.

Maybe a memory is like a prayer.

My mother should've seen a neurologist. But the more people who knew, the harder it was for her to breathe. My father left, but not before I could make a memory of his mustache. If he had been around he would have received the phone calls home from my elementary school teachers:

"Your daughter forgot to tie her shoes and fell on the concrete. Her knees are only a bit skinned, but she says she's never heard of Wednesday. We need you to come down here and calm her."

"Your daughter fell on the playground again. She's been inconsolable in the cafeteria. She think it's Tuesday and is demanding to know what we've done with the chicken nuggets. We need you to come down here and calm her."

"Your daughter poked through her diorama with a pair of scissors, and cut her hand. She now says she's never read *The Diary of Anne Frank* but she'd been building Frank's cardboard apartment for the last two hours. We need you to come down here and calm her."

If our mother couldn't come right away, the teachers learned to find Ben somewhere in the halls. Even if he was behind the back dumpsters smoking a cigarette or in a backseat with a girl who was about to give in, they'd find him. He'd sit with me in the bathroom. He learned to carry Chiclets in his pockets; I never forgot how much I loved Chiclets. Never the white ones. Only the green.

We never told the teachers. They were perplexed, but the physicals each year showed nothing out of joint. My hearing was good. My eyesight could've been better. I would grow into my legs and forehead.

{Make a memory of me please. Make a memory of me please.}

I tell him I will do everything I can. Just before I scrape the back of my arm against the unfinished picnic table.

To understand
You should
Rip this page

{Hello?}

[Hello?]

{It's Teddy.}

[I know.]

He calls me to remind me of his name. I love him that I have not forgotten.

What if we didn't build monuments in memory of, but we returned to making quilts, knowing the texture of those worn fingertips stitched what now keeps us warm. What if we didn't keep memories underneath the sink, where we thought other people would never think to look, but burned them and then we could remember the burning but we wouldn't have the thing, just the heat of what it was, which everyone tells us will wane. Yes, I think some memories should be burned, not to make them disappear, but to transform them into something we can chose whether or not we want to cling to. This choice. Is it the warmth of what was or that we are that keeps us warm? It is this that matters on this last day.

Flossing is hazardous

Root canals are prescribed

I am thankful for my

Sturdy gums

We were juniors in college when I told Jen and she didn't believe me. She knew things happened, and when they did to call Ben. He had disavowed college for the manufacturing plant where he packed styrofoam plates he called chicken coffins. When our mother died we left the apartment, found a small space off Chapel Street where I could easily get to school and Ben could forget he went to work. Some nights Ben would bring home a twelve pack of Genny Cream Ale, and we'd sit smoking halfheartedly towards the open windows in the winter, talking about what kind of lottery it would've been if my mother and I had sold our stories, sold my story. I'd thought about it. But Ben didn't want me to be a petri dish. Plus what would they do? Those doctors? Oliver Sacks would feature me in his newest paperback, through some tagline on the cover, like *The Woman Whose Brain Made Band-Aids From Her Past*, and the affliction that will ruin my life would tickle his beard in his townhouse, while I'd still not remember where the bathroom was if I rubbed off the back of my heels wearing a new pair of shoes.

So I immersed myself safely in the quilt of fiction and poets who wrote about tributaries of lost memories, and felt better when Russell Edson wrote, "But then there is fiction, so that one is never really sure if it was someone who / vanished into the end of seeing, or someone made of paper and ink…" because it meant that these pages in your hands could be a way to keep me huddled in her head, and she could remember to keep me with her, and think of me as made from leaves. Lyn Hyjenian was right too: this writing is an aid to memory. This what you are reading now is. But when Tony Hoagland wrote: "Friends, we should have postmarks on our foreheads / to show where we have been," I know better. What if the stamp is all that's there. No envelope, no letter beneath, just the stamp. This would frighten you, I'm sure. But maybe then you could understand.

Ways to Lose

Using a knife to pick something out of something
Eating tortilla chips
Unfinished picnic tables
Emptying the crumbs out of the toaster
Ripping a hangnail
Flossing with a piece of found cardboard
So many things scissors can do
A piece of hamburger with metal in it
All kinds of slivers
Knuckles on accident across a grater
Poorly upholstered furniture
Reaching into any number of things
Pulling the aluminum foil across the blade carelessly
A stapled finger
A tongue rubbed rough against the inside of a soda can

Teddy makes presentations for supermarkets. Brochures so that Safeway will purchase a new line of utopian self-checkouts. Powerpoint presentations on how to handle the most recent pistachio recall. A website for the Asparagus Club Golf Tournament held during the National Grocers Association Annual Convention. Sometimes when we used to get drunk I would tell him how sad the policing of counterfeit coupons made me.

Maybe for me, what you're reading with me, what you're paging through too quickly as I write it, is a way to break with some ugly histories. An invitation to creation. Like how we appeal to others' remembrances to make ourselves. Because we can imagine our past when we can't remember it. When we forget we play dress up with others' memories. Can a life be a fraud like a coupon? Is a close likeness of life enough for a life?

We'd like to believe it could never be but it is. We are living a portrait of our lives. Not our lives. This is what I tell myself to believe. It's not true. Not remembering the face of the person whose hand you hold is not an invitation, an opportunity to make the portrait different. Not remembering the man lying next to you, or the friend as she walks down the aisle, because of a car accident, this is not an invitation. It is not an appeal. It is a howl. A protest against the portrait you can't remember.

Signs of Memory Loss

Using too many adjectives
Relying on written notes
Abandoning a budget
Passing a mirror and thinking
Someone else is in the room
Confusing seasons
Insisting orange is a verb
Accusing someone of stealing
When was the last time you bathed?
Calling a watch a hand-clock
Giving money to telemarketers
An inability to admit mistakes
Leaving the iron in the freezer

There are signs of memory loss that don't seem right.

Using too many adjectives:
Maybe William Carlos Williams was right to keep his *Spring and All* so quiet, to almost refuse its existence. Three hundred copies distributed, forgotten until after his death and now it's not difficult to find someone who knows of a contagious hospital. The flowers in his poems are pink confused white reversed shaded. Williams and his baffled adjectives. Maybe he had problems with his hippocampus.

An inability to admit mistakes:
Maybe Williams was right to think that jackass T.S. Eliot was such a quack, an obstinate fool who spent his life refusing. Though, to be sure, Williams could've been more sensitive about the brain injury Eliot might've had.

But in *Paterson* Williams says memory is "a kind of accomplishment / a sort of renewal / even / an initiation, since the spaces it opens are new places." He was wrong then. Memory is not like a new lawn. Those new places know they are not new because of the looks on the faces of friends and lovers who wish they would not need to remind you of those special times that no cut should have ever taken away.

My impoverished brain and I. I wish I could feel them leaving. If only memories had textures, like rough fabric against the palm of your hand. They could be between my fingers and then float away but there would still be the ink, like what a newspaper leaves, an impression of friction, an epidermal ridge, a print. How our fingertips are built into our senses, like how our senses are built into our memory, so are built into our fingertips. But instead there is only the empty.

The last time Teddy and I drove past the apartment building where Ben and I grew up, it wasn't there.

What it's like to remember a place that doesn't exist. What it's like to forget a place that never existed, only to be surprised that it still doesn't exist. Where is the stair that creaks in the house that's no longer there?

In my hands is the blueprint of a life that is no longer mine.

The couch on our enclosed porch. I can still smell the upholstery of a thing that was taken to the dump a decade ago. The tight writhing of our senses and our memory.

In my mind I'm sure I can and that I've never needed to be reminded.

At least it's not from syphilis. There's that piano player, who VD did this to, who keeps a journal where he writes that he feels like every time he wakes up it's the first time he's ever woken up. Everyone thinks there's something to this that might not be so terrible.

What if our memory could be mapped? These pages. See them as a road atlas. Latitudes of previous breaths. 435 miles until we're finally out of Colorado. The local roads as senses: Routes 5 & 20 could be the wedding present sheets after their first wash; Route 332 my nose into the crook of Teddy's neck; I-90: Teddy asked me to marry him; I-81: the squash salad at the reception that seemed like a good idea but no one ate, not even Jen and Gary. A life with an unauthenticated compass of lines. What's in the legend: but it seemed like marrying in a church was the right thing to do, like a good luck charm, like having our wedding in those old stones would be a rabbit's foot in my pocket.

What ideogram could possibly represent Teddy like a mast at the end of the aisle? Could a turnpike represent: everything descended the way it should afterwards: that game of "Slap the Bag" when friends fell down drunken and we wished them a good night as they got into their cars then went straight to sleep, so happy there weren't any incidents. Of the fewer than fifteen of us present, only Jen, Gary, Teddy, and I knew what could've happened can't be shown on a map.

Now. Think of the quotidian in your brain. Think of it as a pulsating sock from which holes in the toes sprout the names Nim Chimpsky or Project Pigeon, B.F. Skinner's plot to put missiles on pigeons. Think of hysterical strength and the feats of the father of your sixth-grade teacher who lifted the family station wagon off her sometime before you were born. These are the memories that fight for space with the way Teddy's leg twitches when he's near-sleep.

There's the Jack Gilbert poem "Highlights and Interstices" which I can recite from heart but rarely do. Others of Gilbert's lines about keeping in mind the way mothers help their children across the street without thinking, the way they reach for a hand, the way a hand reaches for them. That it is what is between the memorable that matters.

Here's how it works: knowing this poem I can recite from memory, which celebrates the every day, means that it might not be forgotten while some version of my own every day might leave me: Teddy always lets me check the mail, I'm allergic to Christmas trees, Sunday is the best day of the week

Sometimes when I'm upset with Teddy I memorize poems to punish myself. I'll probably never forget James Tate's "Fuck the Astronauts": "Eventually we must combine nightmares / an angel smoking a cigarette on the steps / of the last national bank, said to me."

That James Tate could stay when my birthday would need to leave so I could scab properly.

There is this advantage: I enjoy over and over the same good things for the first time.

Teddy leaves me a note in a drawer underneath underthings:

There is this advantage: Crossed bridges burned in rearviews. Nothing to show of blunders. Not even the smell of smoke Teddy left me a note inside a pillowcase:

There is this advantage: the palest ink is better than the best. Teddy left me a note in my pocket:

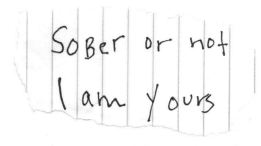

One time on the bus I wrote:

Does God have a ~~head injury a nasty streak of bile for a heart for~~.
Memory can it be ~~a bottlecap found in a pocket, an electrical char~~ge.
A throat passage ~~through an unlit supermarket spoiled fruit.~~
In the vamp of a shoe ~~the throat line of hope and insole of tragedy.~~
Hateful island of things ~~marooned in a communal present.~~
Abbreviated inbetweens ~~that can disappoint more than the weather~~
Of happenings.

One time Jen told me something she'd never told anyone, and
afterwards, asked me if we could prick my finger so that I might not
remember it. It didn't work. The prick took something else. Because I
still remember. This was the only time she asked me. I would've tried
again.

Before me Teddy was with someone else. Of course he was with someone else. I knew her. She didn't know me but she knew me. We had beers and she thought I was weird one night when I left quickly after biting the inside of my lip on accident, afraid I might forget the way home. They ended before Teddy and I began but she's always still there I feel her.

Now I sometimes become uncontrolled. When he talks to her again. When he tells me he cares about her. {Why can't I care about her?} He can't tell me he cares about her because he knows that I can't forget that he does. I'm convinced that because of this he can't not think about her. She is taller and could have his baby and she knows to touch his arm in the way he likes. He doesn't tell me about the picture of her underneath the sink in a paper bag. The one that I dream about burning. There they are. Those two in the backyard together. Does he keep the picture there so he finds it accidentally every few Tuesdays, so he can sit in his mind, in a ratty chair on that lawn that was theirs, in that moment when it is his arm at her back. She is there. It is fall and they share a house and they have raised an ugly dog and they wear rings on the wrong fingers but they wear rings. There they are. She is in his mind like walking; he cannot forget how to walk and she will be there with him when he does look underneath the sink. She is fuller and would make him better breakfasts and she isn't interesting and because of this she is interesting. Because of what can be lost, what isn't buzzes exposed at all times. I make his memories mine. He says "we" when he means where he used to live where she lived with him and my memory of his memories stings. It is excruciating. It won't go away. No matter how hard I might floss she and he are not what will disappear. That cleave means to make faithful and to penetrate a split. There are enough reasons for contronyms to make their way back in. That cleave could mean to make as if by cutting.

{But your nose was pierced when we met?}

{You don't just have baby teeth?}

{But you shave your legs?}

{What if you needed a new appendix?}

{What if you bit your lip?}

{Even paper cuts?}

                    [Even Christmas-card-envelope-licking tongue cuts.]

{Do you know which ones you've lost?}

                                        [How could I?]

{Does this mean we'll never have a baby?}

[We'll never have a baby.]

{Undo your pants.}

{Start with the top button.}

Now is the time for pants,
but I comply. Now is the time
for bedlam. But so much
softer. So much
slower.

The night I told him, I waited for his response was to move to the bed. Mattress migrating from the wall, no headboard to hold it in place, hands reaching behind to hold onto something, hands reaching above to feel more, to make imprints, in skin, on synapses, it can't go hard enough, it can't last this hard enough.

A pillow case on the floor. Sheets strewn. Teddy's got one black sock. I've got nothing. This is not an inbetween. My foot reaches for the instep of his. Involuntarily. Perspiring. Teddy lying half on me, me half-not-breathing. He's on me and he's pink everywhere.

Afterwards, we adjusted, lay side by side together on the bed, evidence of what's left would show on those dark sheets.

After we had caught our breaths we held them.

Teddy wondering what we were supposed to do next.
I wondering what we had just done.

Teddy knows. Plugs a phone in. He waits.

Wonders if I will answer. Teddy knows.

I cannot forget the sound.

Teddy does not know.

If next time I will remember his name.

We will only know the joy of raising turtles. Little
rogues. We will care for them.

I cut myself washing dishes butter knife in the
disposal.

If you ripped this page
you would know.

If only a moon could flood my memory, polish it, burn it into my colon, someplace that's less required than my mind.

~~I notice a spot. Someone once said he loved only what a person wrote~~
~~with her own blood Frantic. At first. I am. Swatting. Yes. I remember~~
~~how~~ it began. ~~I remember her. Yes. At a horsefly. I was swatting.~~ With
~~something to prick it in my han~~ds.

~~These things happen sometimes. There's been similar incidents. Now~~
~~there~~ is ~~an inflammation and a bit of wet and a severed tendon. No.~~
~~Not yet. A bandage underneath a sleeve will keep him from worrying.~~
~~But Teddy doesn't worry anymore. If I severed a tendon~~ I might never
remember ~~his name. Because I cannot expect what I will forget~~.

~~It couldn't be worse.~~
~~How do you know what you've forgotten?~~

~~Sometimes, for you, there's that imprint, when sometimes just the~~
~~shadow that engram once cast in your cortex something is~~ enough ~~to~~
~~make you remember when you run into Jen to tell her that last week you~~
~~remembered when you recited Bernadette Mayer's "You jerk you didn't~~
~~call me up" when her boyfriend before her husband fucked her over~~
~~and there you were, you two, drinking wine straight from the bag and~~
~~repeating over and over again "You can either make love or die at the~~
~~hands of / the Cobra Commander". This is the tracing ribbon you cling~~
~~to. Something encoded in your mind provides a clue. You can cling to.~~
~~When you see a picture of your fifth grade classroom (yes, that's you in~~
~~the blue jumper, the plastic glasses so heavy you tipped your head, the~~
~~tinted acne cream that never matched your winter tan, all these as you~~
~~lean self-consciously into the pupil next to you in the hopes that you'll~~
~~remember wrong that that was a good year and you'll remember wrong~~
~~that you did get invited and she was loved her present) reminds you of~~
~~the way your mother smelled like salisbury steaks then. Remembering~~
~~wrong is still remembering.~~

We reconstruct lives; we do not record them faithfully. Or we do neither. After he burned the Temple of Artemis, the Ephesus leaders ordered Herostratus' name never to be spoken again. Damnatio memoriae. If we remember to not speak it aren't we remembering it? Sometimes memory is just noise and a life like an abyss, where I wait, with Joseph Ceravolo, "for the masonry / to show a little slit / for my soul to get through."

During the April tornado outbreak:

In the vortex that was that year. 148 tornadoes. 13 states. Most averaged six miles. Most averaged less than fifteen minutes. Carnage, Xenia, Ohio, can be remembered but is no longer there. Someone recorded a wind scream from near the inside of one. Ground so hot warm air bursts. Pregnant swimming winds. Even volcanoes seem more egalitarian in their location and what is lost. Archetypal Disaster. The most destructive, their scientific term: incredible. Cars seized and bucked and spun into darkness. These were the ones that lasted longer. Some meteorologist said we saw the power of creation.

During the April tornado outbreak:

I stretched my panties so when he tugged they'd rip quicker.

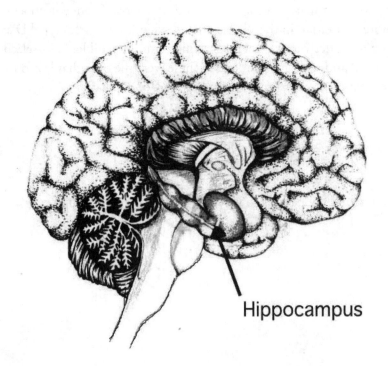

Hippocampus

We need this part that looks like a kidney connected to a thwarted sausage to create connections; there is where I first find out about my mother's condition, on the jungle gym in the city park near our apartment, on the swing where my mother pushes me tells me her brain makes her unhappy she is sorry it hurts when she doesn't remember whether or not I'm allergic to certain festive trees. It is the hippocampus that makes me recall that day smelled like it was snowing someplace else. The chain of the swing became cold as the front moved into the last week of September when the heat wouldn't be turned on yet. I remember thinking that if we didn't go inside we wouldn't realize we were cold.

Unlike my mother, I went to see a neurologist once. I didn't say anything about this affliction; I don't wear my hippocampus on my sleeve. He said the role of the hippocampus had been demystified. We think in patterns. Our past is a pattern made of diamonds in diagonal checkerboard arrangements.

I feel like I know so much better than the scientists sometimes memories can't be kept in tight squares of ash and fire.

Everyone else has a functional structure to their memory; my mother and I, our timelines interrupted. She couldn't, and I still can't, stitch together the disparate.

It takes two missed times of the month for me to run into a Rite-Aid and buy the generic version of the test that tells me what I know to be true. Sitting in the bathroom of a Wendy's, I wonder how to tell Teddy I might become a mother.

[This is where we will be next.]

The decision I should've made wasn't the one I would make. I order off the menu I can afford and think about what being pregnant means. Not that I might bring into the world yet another person with too much plaque on her teeth who tried never bite her lip and looked cautiously at rough sawn wood at Home Depot. But someone who would remember what I sang. On other continents, they ask foreigners to sing a song from the homeland. If I had a son, he could sing how he goes home not to memory but salted hot chocolate. When I have a daughter, she will sing of Hart Crane and everyone will wonder with her "how much room for memory there is / in the loose girdle of soft rain."

At home Teddy begs me to think it over. He doesn't know how it works. He knows there will be damage. He worries I am ignoring repercussions. I tell him my mother forgot her name before she held me for the first time. [But she still held me.] {But there were studies once, of giving certain drugs to pregnant women that would make them forget the pain of childbirth, so much so that they forgot the act of and what they held in their arms afterwards felt foreign.} I tell him twilight sleep doesn't happen anymore, that it won't happen to me. That too much has already been lost and that I want to make new. I want to create something that will sing to me and then Maybe I will never forget. I can tell he's not convinced, but he can't keep himself from wondering what's beneath my belly. He is entranced. He will be convinced.

While pregnant I become

the opposite of worrying; I become the may-fly is the most careless fly
that dances; not *not* taking due care; but my bad habits continue; I can
sometimes hide them underneath the patio; I would go to Mexico to
keep them; they won't smoke themselves; I will not give them up in the
night; I tell Teddy [They are the aesthetic equivalent of entropy.]; he
says {Their fixity is not absurd but unfair.}; he is strong and worried; I
am frustrated that he follows me down the stairs; I tell him *he* is unfair;
a nail is driven out by another nail; I enjoy gardening; hate lawn care;
Teddy will not allow me to drive the mower; he says it is too dangerous
a cut that deep might take away; at first I agree; I must keep myself in
order; for him I kept myself in order for a time; the fox changes his skin
but not his skin. I pick at my fingernail until from skin I rip a piece of
nail attached.

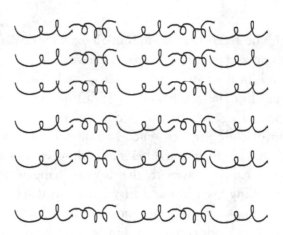

I cannot forget I am pregnant.

I AM INV

INCIBLE

Paranoid in the early afternoons ~~when I am swollen and worried~~
Before the snow when he gets home ~~I am more careful than I let on~~
We keep one foot near the radiator ~~for what's warm leaves a mark as we~~
Lie alongside each other

My innocent spouse
Until it begins to snow
We are invincible

Twenty Weeks In

I'm needing
things: sour apples, vinegar.

I remember dreaming
of having a kid when I was a kid
and naming her Jordache.

My joints
slip, my limbs I tell them
not to float away.

After the ultra-
sound Teddy says she's
the size of a beer bottle.

Six months in I lean across the end of the bed, in slow motion step quietly into the cold morning, but Teddy still wakes.

{Where you going?}

[It's Ben's birthday, gotta give him a call.]

Teddy pauses. Says my name. Reaches from beneath the covers to hold my hand and tug me back to bed. He touches my face. Says his name. I have not forgotten. I have grown to hate him when he does this because it's often to tell me something I can remember. What it's like when Teddy tells me there is something to remember that I'm not remembering.

[It's Ben's birthday.]

{Ben is dead.}

Time slows down and segments into separate moments. The despair that must be felt. Again. That Teddy is wrong. I would never forget Ben dying.

There is the fact that I forgot that Ben is dead.

Then there is the different kind of despair: Teddy's. He has to tell me the bad news again. He has to see me relive. He has to pick me up off the floor. This is the way we live. How can I really hold it against him when he leaves? Is it unfair if it is true? He tells me he was the one to tell me what happened to Ben when it happened. Three years ago, apparently. He says he went to the funeral. He will go with me to Ben's grave again. We will put a pinwheel near him that would've made Ben cringe if he could cringe. But there's another despair too. That Teddy has created a memory that could disappear. Again.

I search my hands for marks, my elbow to see if skin was split, my ankles. But there is nothing.

Teddy puts his hand on top of mine, takes it to the top of my head which I now remember hitting against the edge of the cupboard last night as I looked for the peanut butter. I tell myself to be more careful. I touch the part of me that swells that reminds me to be more careful. I have weathered something. Been exposed and gone safely through.

Alone in the shower, I grieve again. Even as I promise to become more careful I sometimes wish for specific cuts.

If I never remember Ben dying does Ben never die?

You. Do it. Rip this page.

Memory begins before birth. A fetus learns to be familiar with noises. At first these disturbances accelerate her heart rate. But if exposed to them again and again she will no longer react. My daughter hears Teddy scold me all day.

{Don't handle the recycling, the edge of the aluminum could do damage.}

{Don't load the knives that way into the dishwasher.}

{If you pick at your hangnails you know what will happen.}

{We shouldn't eat tortilla chips anymore. What if you scrape the roof of your mouth?}

He's working from home now. He wants to be here to touch my stomach and to supervise the way I cut my bagel. She will be born ignoring her father's stern words. We touch my stomach softly. We are both afraid.

Teddy loves to watch me evolve. He wants to talk to her and tell her not to be afraid. He does not say of what.

Teddy decides our daughter will not be afflicted. He says he willed it to be so. My pregnancy has made him desperate. He is exposed. Everything about him is heightened in a way that I wonder if he's doing these things because he thinks I'll have less of a chance of forgetting.

We hope for first-degree rips during her birth. Small nicks. Uninteresting abrasions. I've been told they usually heal quickly and cause little to no discomfort. But the women who told me don't know about me.

We tell the doctor we need to steer clear of an episiotomy.

We tell the doctor caesarean is not an option. A surgical incision could spell disaster.

We hope that the room I have for her there will be enough to encourage her arrival.

The doctor tells me my body will cut itself in the way it needs to make room. She promises not to.

While making Teddy dinner one night I bump my knuckles
the wrong way on the cheese grater.

Teddy would
want you to rip
this page while I
watch.

~~I notice a spot. Someone once said he loved only what a person wrote with her own blood Frantic. At first. I am. Swatting. Yes. I remember how~~ it began. ~~I remember her. Yes. At a horsefly. I was swatting.~~ With ~~something to prick it in my hand~~s.

~~These things happen sometimes. There's been similar incidents. Now there~~ is ~~an inflammation and a bit of wet and a severed tendon. No. Not yet. A bandage and sutures, a doctor will keep him from worrying But Teddy doesn't worry anymore. If I severed a tendon~~ I ~~might never~~ remember ~~his name. Because I cannot expect what I will forget.~~

~~It couldn't be worse.~~
~~How do you know what you've forgotten?~~

~~Sometimes, for you, there's that imprint, when sometimes just the shadow that engram once cast in your cortex something is~~ enough to ~~make you remember when you run into Jen to tell her that last week you remembered when you recited Bernadette Mayer's "You jerk you didn't call me up" when her boyfriend before her husband fucked her over and there you were, you two, drinking wine straight from the bag and repeating over and over again "You can either make love or die at the hands of / the Cobra Commander". This is the tracing ribbon you~~ cling to. ~~Something encoded in your mind provides a clue. You can cling to. When you see a picture of your fifth grade classroom (yes, that's you in the blue jumper, the plastic glasses so heavy you tipped your head, the tinted acne cream that never matched your winter tan, all these as you lean self consciously into the pupil next to you in the hopes that you'll remember wrong that that was a good year and you'll remember wrong that you did get invited and she was loved her present) reminds you of the way your mother smelled like salisbury steaks then. Remembering wrong is still remembering.~~

What I forget is a chigger. What I forget exists for those who remember.
It forms a hole in their inner skin, the true skin, more than an irritation.

Chiggers do not burrow, but insert their mouthparts into the skin. Dissolve tissues, digest them. Any camper or barefoot third-grader knows they exist until the first frost. And they itch like hell.

We are told they only cause grief and discomfort. Scratching them removes them from the skin and they die. They will never be the subject of a thousand poems.

The treaty of Westphalia ended the Thirty Years' War and required opposing sides to forgive and forget.

Life is horizontal. Not vertical. We should not stretch backwards to be.

Teddy learns that turtles' organs don't break down. Their livers don't become less efficient. Their lungs at 130 years are their lungs when they've just become their shells. We decide that Owen's longevity is like mine. Owen and I can withstand. When I've forgotten my telephone number I will look to Owen.

Teddy is angry when he sees what I've been grating.
I am swollen and tired and have not forgotten his name.
I tell him:

[Infant chimpanzees have a memory
much better than any human's.]

{By stepping over an object even a cat
can make a memory of it that lasts.}

[The Piraha people whistle
their words. They have
no history besides their living
memory in the present.]

I tell him:
[Memory of a thing is not knowing a thing.]

He finally says quietly:
{But when is it not all we have?}

Teddy doesn't understand that I know that it's what's behind the couches that's the first to go when I get cut: the Snoopy electric toothbrush for an early Christmas spent in footed pajamas, gourmet jellybeans, the names of Jupiter's Galilean moons that aren't Io, Europa, and Ganymede, that friend from the seventh grade shoplifting peanut butter cups before we snuck into *The Last of the Mohicans*.

The brain changes when we make a memory. It's supposed to be burned into. But there isn't heat in the brain from this branding, from those electrical impulses that supposedly happen. So what of the engram, that hypothetical permanent change in the brain that should show a memory's existence?

If we can't observe where a memory was, how can we ever hope to find where it went?

It turns out everyone has amnesia. None of us knows who we were before we were four. It's infantile: we can't describe with words events that occurred in our lives before we knew the words to describe them. This makes it seem that words are why we have memories. Does this mean then, when you forget your words, you become more like me?

I've forgotten Gary before. Two years ago the kind of dog that shivers in the winter bit me on the hand. I needed 10 stitches and we wondered if I'd be able to bend my middle right finger again.

Somehow all I lost was Gary. We didn't know it; while we waited in the emergency room, Teddy tried to figure out what I'd forgotten.

Questions Teddy Asks Me After a Cut and The Correct Answers

{What is my name?} [Teddy]
{What is your sign?} [Aries]
{What is the last line of "somewhere I have never travelled, gladly"} ["nobody, not even the rain, has such small hands"]
{What is your favorite body part of mine?} [That place where the shoulder bone dips]

Odd Questions Teddy Asks Me After a Cut and The Correct Answers

{Who is Indiana Jones named after?} [George Lucas' dog]
{Why would we ever go to Kansas?} [Dinosaur bones]

We didn't know to wonder whether I'd forgotten Gary until a few weeks later. Jen walked into our house with him and a bottle of something and we embraced and I introduced myself.

And no one said anything. So Jen just introduced him. And now? Now I'm remembering when I didn't remember. It's like there are these dirt roads in my brain, and sometimes they're washed away when the sky opens, but even then everyone out in the country finds an alternate way to get to town.

Not every memory is completely erased. I did remember Gary. Because he married Jen eleven years ago. He just looked so much older. That's the thing that makes this not so bad, sometimes makes me not that different from you: if I get a paper cut I might forget that time Teddy and I went on that four-hour drive to get a jar of pickles across the state line, but I don't forget Teddy. Because our memories aren't sequestered in one location: they're spread across like interstates and those unnamed roads in Eastern Europe when Teddy and I were there, a place where people only know to tell you to take your third right and if you're not paying attention you'll end up at a nunnery on accident where the frocked make grain alcohol. But you can usually find your way back.

Gary was surprised I'd forgotten him, but he said he understood. He has Jen. Teddy can't be this way. Because I'm what he has. And I think he's worried mostly because he doesn't want me to forget that not everything has been a brother out a window or a mother who brought home a real Christmas tree.

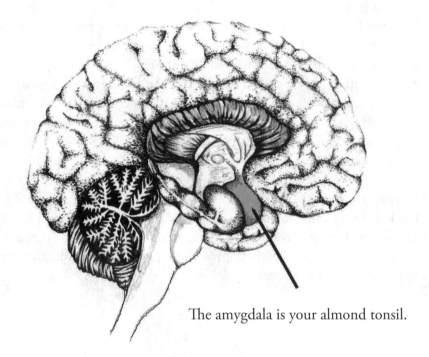

The amygdala is your almond tonsil.

Here is where you remember how to feel about what you remember. Behind your eyebrows your life consolidates. The more emotions you give to events, the more you'll remember them. Here is where it is decided for you what's important enough to store. It is because of this place in your brain you are afraid. Your amygdala works against you-- sending hormones coursing through whenever you see a set of fingers near the door handle of the Taurus weeks after you slammed them. But the words fear and revere are conjoined by origin. This means the rest of your brain might not come to your aid even if it could. Soft, helpless tissue, waiting with breathless anticipation to see what will happen next.

There is memory. And there is emotional memory. One is your phone number. The other is the way your daughter smells.

I tell Teddy I once had a dollhouse because I know he will then go to the store because he wouldn't have thought to get one. When someone says memory is a scaffold, that's when they're nearest to it. Something temporary to hold. Those who find it unsettling aren't wrong. Who wants to watch their loved one hover above the earth to replace a window? But if it's the only way, we'll find a way to deal. We'll pretend our partner is hovering ignorant of physics. Teddy's worry about having a daughter is temporary like that kind of gravity. He will find his way to friendship necklaces and bras that aren't bras yet and halloween costumes of lace floating over legs. He'll pretend he always knew and that the ground was always in sight.

Diseases of Pregnancy

I drool.
Sympathy of organs: the pressure of her on them.
No treatment reliable.
For every child a tooth. An old lady in the waiting room of our
obstetrician's office tells this joke. Teddy squeezes my hand. We know
it is not true. We know that if it were true we would worry.
Restless nausea. Some days so much so I wish she would just
arrive. Barley water. Arrow root.
A collective memory of childbirth: everyone thinks they understand.
That they know.
A nervous system more susceptible to impressions
{Please please please don't be a bruise.}
(Please please please just be a bruise.}

                                        is what she hears.

We must form more blood when I'm pregnant.
Constipation.

Memory refuses time, its indefinite progress, its specific moment. It freezes the image we have of the people we love in a no-time, an ether of remembrance that is both poignant and unfortunate. Teddy says his parents will always be 32-years-old. He does not remember their struggle but the full heads of hair and only a decade of post-collegiate weight gain. I am not unlike him. My mother will always wear her glasses. Ben's hands will always be red and chafed from handling the plates he packed full-time for a decade. Teddy says he hopes I never forget that he had no gut when we met. Those jeans slicking his upper thighs in that way that made me want to be on top of him too often. Now we hold hands more often than doing it in that little Hyundai I had. Time, the tempo of breath, memory, the tide that will eventually take it away.

Teddy wonders if there's something there still, like the fossil of a footprint that proves it left, that if things really can disappear, then something needs to replace what's left me. As if there's an absence begging not to be. I tell him we, you too, we invent everything. Our past. Identity. He says that when I forget we can invent our past together. I wonder whether to tell him that I'm starting to worry whether he wants our past to be sweeter than it was. I do not tell him that wanting to invent me is selfish and he should know better because when we talk about something that's disappeared to mend a bitten lip, he does not tell me about that time in Chicago when we fought and I drank twelve Sierra Nevada Pale Ales and then threw up out the window of my hatchback as we drove his mom to the airport. I think he basks in his role of inventor in control. He tells me instead about the copy of *Cat's Cradle* I got his mom that she loved, and how she underlined a section of the last sentence: "I would make a statue of myself."

Memory is like a neighborhood where what happens on the front porch across the street matters. Take the first moment I knew I loved Teddy: there's the external context next door to the love: the socks he was wearing, that he kept trying to push errant spikes of hair smooth. The internal context across the street: that I was self-conscious about my glasses. That I should've brushed my teeth. That when we laughed about (what was it?) I remember thinking I wanted to dig underneath his--it was his fingernails. I wanted to burrow underneath his fingernails like a preposition.

You can condition yourself to remember a memory in a certain way. Someone can teach you to think of third grade differently. Or hear that Bob Dylan song "Most of the Time" and not cringe like you always do. So that you don't remember the third grade when only the newly acquired names of planets kept you company. Or you could coast through the more painful reminder of your current love who tells you how much he cares about his ex. So that when Dylan sings: "Don't even remember what her lips felt like on mine. Most of the time" you don't wish you could fit your heart into the food processor.

How it Began on a Wednesday

Dilation.
Let it stretch.
Expansion.
Not give way.
Bear down.
She burns.
Breath.
From inside
She sees the inside of my hip.
I remember "I can't" always palsies. "I will"
Will aid delivery.
I think "I am not different from anyone else."
She descends.
Rotates to glance behind me.
I think "I am adapted for this."
She is looking backwards before she becomes.
They turn her once more.
The doctor doesn't know of my condition.
I can hear her.
If anyone knew.
I can hear her.
She will not become a petri dish.
She is.

I have not forgotten anything I can remember.

What happens when they cut the cord?
If she is like me.
The placenta weighs six pounds.
Will she have to begin again?
Let the placenta have cloaked my affliction from her.
What if she loses Teddy reading Pogo to her all these months?
The placenta and its structure of trees.
Will she never remember that
{"whichever pair of trousers you put on in the morning, that's
who you are for that particular day."}

Long awaited wrong ~~choice made perfect by evolution's insistent~~
choice in my arms ~~that reach for her reaching for me an instin~~ct
this must be the place a ~~landscape of senses drifts of the moment~~ous
I will keep these ~~fingers her jitters her cries that mouth my name~~
shining parts ~~the cuts that will come will come and will cut us both~~
but the cuts.

At Cornell they decide that turtles always know where they are and where they are going. Female turtles return to the beaches where they were born to give birth to new turtles. They always know where they are from. This is like how a man with amnesia, who doesn't know how beautifully he sings, tries for the first time to hit a minor chord, and makes a perfect note. Teddy tells me that even if I misuse the stapler, even if I finally have to floss, there are things I will never forget. If I don't have a natal beach, that is alright, we decide. Our daughter will be my beach. And I will always know her. Because of this we make love unconcerned about making another. For at least a few weeks we decide we could always be.

On Subtraction

Of the principles
It is founded
I acquiesce
The inverse of what
I've just done
Is to withdraw
From the whole
None of the burdens

Right now. You're the only other one who knows.
Rip this page so I won't.

THIS IS WHY IT BEGINS

Consider this. In your hands. My external memory. I've turned
the invisible things I carry with me into this. These pages
in your hands. Exist because I don't want her to mistrust her memory.

Like I do mine. Because this is all I have of her name:

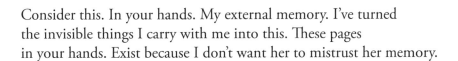

On the morning she was born Teddy and I paid specific attention to the weather. We wanted to be able to tell her everything about the moments just before she arrived, what the wind was doing, how the trees were receiving it, whether it felt wet or dry or if the air knew she was coming too and so it tried hard to be the kind of perfect inbetween where everyone wants to be on a covered porch or close to the window. Then it started to rain as we walked into the hospital and we wondered, how are we going to tell her about this? Then the temperature dropped thirty degrees in a matter of minutes while we waited for the paperwork and it began to snow.

And it was beautiful. Or it wasn't; it was cold and a November-like-fall instead of a September-like-fall. Except Teddy remembered: when you think the weather is bad you're more likely to remember. This is a fact. Look it up.

Semantic memory: apples can be green. San José is the capital of Costa Rica. There was a Thirty Years' War. A wrench could be a pet and a tool. I have given birth. I slammed my finger in the door of the Taurus and called a cab home and never drove again. Left the verb means to have gone. Left the adjective means remaining. To have gone but still remain. Or what's remaining has already left.

Frank Lloyd Wright said belief in a thing makes it be. That truth is more important than fact.

The truth is she will be like me. The fact is her father will know what to do. The truth is she could forget me.

Since she arrived Teddy is entranced. On the drive home from the hospital he didn't roll one stop. He has become a father. He is farther than who he's been. Farther from me. He thinks she will never forget his name. His amygdala doesn't force him to make a phone ring. He is always on the verge of ugly disappointment toward me, wondering when I am going to do something foolish and hurt our daughter with what I forget. His patience with me is losing its grip. I hope we will stay upright through it. This is all I can do.

I look in on my daughter ~~and the undulating prairie of life she will be~~
Touch her fingers wonder ~~about the impracticality of her perfection~~
Watch them clutch[2] ~~attempt at control and warmth and being near~~
Her body will forget this reflex ~~this should scare no one, it happens~~
On its own.
Right now she holds tight.

I will fend off her every cut

2. When an object is placed in the hand of an infant the fingers close over it out of reflex. This having also been observed in the case of an infant born without a brain, one might interpret it as normally taking place without brain cooperation. Still. I think she grasps because she knows. Right now.

She knows.

Until she will forget.

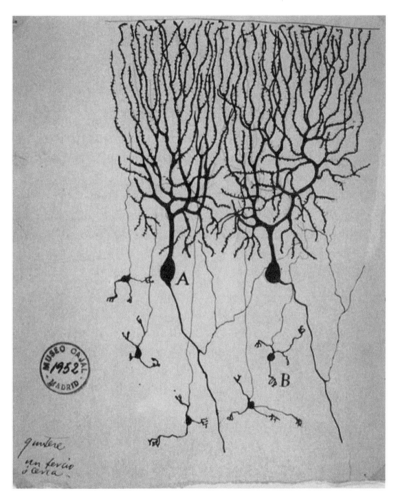

These are the cells in our brains and here is where we move because we learned sequences. In 1837, the Czech physiologist Purkinje discovered where it is that makes us master a particular task we haven't reflected on, like walking. So he drew us an image of how we take breaths. When we have them left.

Frank Lloyd Wright says to me in a dream like he did to someone else:

"An architect's most useful tools are an eraser at the drafting board, and a wrecking bar at the site."

The Gordon Strong Automobile Objective. Designed but never built. Is a blueprint a belief like a memory. Did the Gordon Strong Automobile Objective never exist?

Frank changed his middle name from Lincoln to Lloyd. Some people want to forget. His father sued his mother in the divorce. For lack of physical affection.

The Gordon Automobile Objective. You see it. On this page. But it never existed. Though you could remember it now. It didn't have to be built to be ███████.

Mine is not a dissociative fugue in which people lose their identity and become a not-someone, a person with no-past. Those people can't remember anything. Most people recover from their fugue; they eventually find what wasn't there. It just happens. They wonder why they have a mustache and then they look in the mirror the next day and remember: Teddy grew that mustache as my birthday present.

A fugue opens with one voice, one subject. Others join in. But the subject stays the same. It is a flight. To flee from what. This was the simple subject of Bach's last fugue.

But the fugue ends abruptly when Bach dies. Some people think it was a choice. Left open for others to put together. Like this. What you are reading now. Is a choice. For you and she to put together.

The first time it happened she bumped her head against the fireplace we hadn't made safe. She looked at me. I didn't know if she forgot my name. When I tried to feed her peas that night, she didn't make a face, didn't remove them from her mouth with her delicious fat fingers. She had forgotten she didn't like peas.

A hoped for therapeutic forgetting.

You
Rip this
For her

Jen was in the hospital with us when she was born. While Teddy paced, Jen held my hand. When they did have to make incisions to make room for her to arrive, Jen held tighter. For the first time I think she was afraid for me. There I was covered in the things delivering women are covered with and Teddy's doing his best:

{You can do it. You can do it.}

And then she arrives. And we all realize we're not sure what I've forgotten, but it's nothing that's with us in the room. We all know I've gotten away with something. What this means for each of us is different; I'm the only one who thinks there will be a price to pay.

Scientists say forgotten things reduce demands on the brain. They don't though. Scientists say certain memories are crowded out to make room for what's important.

There is an island to be found, always. That day we walked in the field together, with the Polaroid camera, where the weeds outran the grass, a day when the trees reached for me, six months before she was born. And I was still invincible. And it smelled like it might be summer forever.

There will always be places insulated.

So nobody's marooned in the present. Not even me.

When he's writing about architecture Frank Lloyd Wright quotes Coleridge: "Such as the life is, such is the form."

Teddy. I don't tell you, but now I think we only belong together like mutually aligned urinals on a wall.

Our daughter is here and Teddy no longer adheres to my side. He wants alone moments with her that aren't able to be forgotten. When she has her first smirk he celebrates by himself, burning the instant into a cerebrum safe from my affliction. To him, I was the female animal responsible for her arrival. He lets me sleep through the night not from tender concern, but because he thinks her cries are specific to him. He doesn't remember how used to know me. I am external to him now. His love for me has become vestigial.

After her arrival it takes weeks for me to notice what I've forgotten.
I have never looked at her and not known who she is.
It isn't immediate. This decision.
You and I. As as we read this together as I remember.
If it ever happened, that I looked at her and didn't know her.
I would not survive.

Teddy doesn't leave me alone with our daughter if he can help it. He's forwarded his calls home. He's thirty-six now. Always nervous. Not that I'll nick myself. Not anymore. But that I'll do it near her.

He's lost weight since we brought her home.
Last night he said to me before we put her down:

{I don't feel familiar with my hair.}

He didn't speak directly to me. He talks towards and at me now. It's as though he thinks what the cut takes leaves empty space. And it is growing. Between my ears. That somehow I'm becoming less. He doesn't see me becoming more. Afraid. It's as though he thinks that the last paper cut made me forget long division or why I wish we had a parliamentary system of government. But it's not an absence. I will know what I've forgotten at some point. Sometimes it takes longer to find it, but I will be told I've forgotten and that at least makes a place. Doesn't it?

You. Do you remember when I told you about the man with amnesia who couldn't believe he could sing until he sang?

Being a mother is like not knowing you knew how to play an instrument, and then as soon as she's born you realize you've been playing that instrument your entire life.

Teddy and I. We are also realizing. We can't always be.

Emotions latch themselves onto. Alter the memory each time it's recalled. This is reconsolidation.

When memories are recalled they become malleable.

Teddy tells me I've forgotten that we went to Costa Rica.

He tells me I only got a little sunburnt. And that we saw trees with fur for bark. And we talked about never coming home. But he says this as though even he's having trouble remembering what that was like.

Teddy can make my memory different. I used to remember our trip to Costa Rica. But it disappeared. He fills it back in.

I wonder if what is filled in is not what was. Is a memory a truth. Is a memory a fact.

Teddy traces her hand everyday.
He tracks her rooting reflex: when her cheek is touched she turns her
head and opens her mouth.
He touches her cheek.
She opens her mouth.
He notes this.

We are proud of even
her neck. She raises it
to watch us sit on separate
sides of every room.

Teddy notes that her head bobbles about less now.
I notice and make a joke that she no longer
agrees with everything I say.
Teddy does not note this. That her bobbing
was like nodding.

A Map of My Memory Might Look Like

That a small town television newscaster said a local artist found
inspiration in "remnant plumbing fittings" and I said aloud

        [But she doesn't know what the word "remnant" means.]

A ticket stub to *Richard III*
All the thin slick receipts for cigarettes half-smoked
Pizza crusts eaten with Ranch dressing
Hot pavement on bare feet
Nap fever
That dip between my daughter's nose and mouth like a scoop of sugar
Be a cautious cartographer
I tell myself
When Teddy sleeps on the couch

Cicero says nature teaches us what to remember: we fail to remember banal things because they're not marvelous. But marvelous things, those we can remember. He says a sunrise is marvelous to no one because it happens every day. He wants us to set images, to make them unvague, maybe singularly ugly, so they won't leave us. Because my daughter takes a breath every day. I will make that marvelous. Because Teddy once wanted to wake up with me, I should make this the not-ugly.

This is more difficult to do these days.

Cicero's name comes from the word chickpea. But many people were named after beans then. When his young daughter died, he wrote "I have lost the one thing that bound me to life."

When I think of what would happen if I lost her I say aloud to no one in the room:

[I have lost the one thing that binds me to me.]

Teddy tracks our daughter's moro reflex: her neck arched, her arms and legs thrown back quick and then pulled back to her chest as she cries. She does this when he raises his voice at me. She is two-months-old and soon she will lose the instinct to protect herself from falling when her father raises his voice towards me.

Teddy is trying to track her temporal knowledge in his notes. He says if we talk to her about the future then she will understand the future. He says he thinks she'll know what yesterday means soon. He says her knowledge of the future will come from understanding what's passed. I ask him:

[But what of the present?]

He says:
{Does it even exist?}

Yourself is a concept made by your self. If our memory of who we are is who we are. I refuse. I want to be in the way Descartes says I am. I dragged Teddy's hair out of the sink today. I am. I breast-fed my daughter today. I am.

Locke says we look backwards to be. He is a threat. He believed what I can't remember has no part of what I've become. As if we cannot be defined by what isn't there. Who doesn't hope this isn't true?

There are things I lose sometimes when I shave. And I don't always know what they are. You and I. We must not subscribe to the notion that what we've lost defines us. That without memory we are just a something that responds to stimuli.

Right now I cannot tell Teddy I have forgotten what we had for dinner at our wedding reception. But I remember Hulme. He's the one to believe in. Fuck Locke. Hulme says if we know something must have happened, even if we can't locate it, well then that'll do. We can trust we've been there even if we don't know exactly where we've been.

Reproduce every experience? I cannot. But reconstruct? I can.
Or Teddy can for me, if he wants to, which he doesn't seem to now.

I cannot remember our wedding reception. But that does not make us not married. No matter how things are now.

Except there's who am I when I rely on someone else to reconstruct who I was. Teddy tells me when we met I had a nose ring. This seems likely. Because when we met I couldn't have known how much could be lost.

Forgetting is a humiliated silence for those of us forced to live in the impression of time lost.

In the twelfth Century, Boncompagno da Signa wrote that "all books that have been written ... all paintings ... all crosses, of stone, iron, or wood set up at the intersections of two, three, or four roads ... eye extractions, mutilations, and various tortures of bandits and forgers; all posts that are set up to mark out boundaries ... the blarings of horns and trumpets ... clocks ... the marks and points on knucklebones; varieties of colors, memorial knots, supports for the feet, bandages for the fingers ... small notches that ... stewards make in sticks ... the blows given to boys to preserve the events of history ... the nods and signals of lovers; the whispers of thieves; courteous gifts and small presents -- all have been devised for the purpose of supporting the weakness of natural memory."

This, in your hands, is like all of those.

Scientists have found the more we're told to resist thinking about a word, the more trouble we'll have remembering it later.

I cannot make
a telephone ring
I cannot make

I slammed my finger in the door of the Taurus that day, trying to get her out of the car seat, trying not to lose her father's "I wish I were dead" coffee cup off the roof of the car, while trying to put my keys in my purse. She screamed. I did not. Gritting my teeth in the moment, everything I am just a response to a stimuli. This was a present that I wish moved more quickly to the past.

From the peripheral nerves through the spinal cord to behind my forehead. The pain these electricities produce does not make me afraid. Yet I close my eyes and I see the physicality of my fear as it becomes manifest.

The thalamus. It begins here.

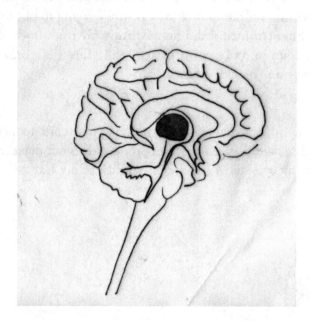

Inputs from the retina, from everywhere but the olfactory, visit here. To scale it should be the size of a walnut but to memory it's importance is different. The thalamus is what filters an instant. A thalamium is an inner room in Green Architecture. The receptacle of a flower is like this part that houses our present. A secret that seems very female, this part that you have too. That my daughter has this too.

These electricities. From thalamus. To amygdala. To hypothalamus. I wait. I will forget something because as soon as I open the car door to retrieve my finger, my body will want to make itself heal. Her screaming, from beneath the belly, sound like they're from something not-her, from something deep within her gut, where there are so many nerves and everything's so complex some people call it the second brain. Even if her first brain can't say my name yet, her second brain knows. Your second brain will not forget.

I hold her as we two-step in the parking lot until she's making only whimpering sounds. I am grateful she's too young to worry too long. We keep dancing in the wrong time, counter-clockwise for what seems like hours. Until I realize I am afraid to put her in the car with me because of what I might not know.

Rip.

This.   Do it for me.

Teddy wants to write down in his notes one day that she has the sitting posture of a young chimp. I tell him

      [Don't compare her to something that hunts its own in troops,
          something that's unsympathetic, that is born to make war.]

Teddy says:
{But they can laugh.}

We stop bickering long enough to remember the last time she squealed. When we put a plum near her and it rolled off the table and before Teddy could stop himself from scolding me not to reach underneath because I would bump my head, she began to snort, suck in air and exhale and make her squeal which at that pitch sounds like the happiest steel on steel, her mouth wider than a drain. At that moment we remember that we forget that neither of us knows if we still love each other.

Teddy leaves the house with her more often now. When he's with her

I cannot make a telephone ring.

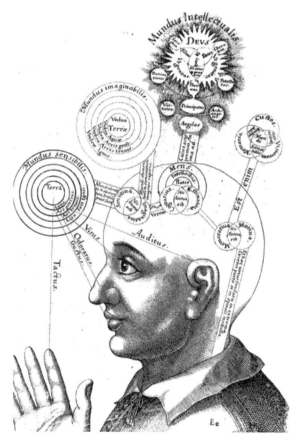

Some time before 1637, Robert Fludd linked memory with our intellect. But also our "motiva" -- our motor systems. This means our spinal cords and our memory are intertwined. This is something I know and that you should remember as you keep reading.

Before this began, when he would take her from me, come back after she was asleep, I'd pick at a fingernail until I ripped the skin to forget.

~~I notice a spot. Someone once said he loved only what a person wrote~~
~~with her own blood Frantie. At first. I am. Swatting. Yes. I remember~~
~~how it began.~~ **I remember** ~~her. Yes. At a horsefly. I was swatting. With~~
~~something to prick it in my hand~~s.

~~These things happen sometimes. There's been similar incidents. Now~~
~~there~~ **is** ~~an inflammation and a bit of wet and a severed tendon. No.~~
Not ~~yet. A bandage underneath a sleeve will keep him from worrying.~~
~~But Teddy doesn't worry anymore. If I severed a tendon I might never~~
~~remember his name. Because I cannot expect what I will forget.~~

~~It couldn't be worse.~~
~~How do you know what you've forgotten?~~

~~Sometimes, for you, there's that imprint, when sometimes just the~~
~~shadow that engram once cast in your cortex something is~~ **enough** ~~to~~
~~make you remember when you run into Jen to tell her that last week you~~
~~remembered when you recited Bernadette Mayer's "You jerk you didn't~~
~~call me up" when her boyfriend before her husband fucked her over~~
~~and there you were, you two, drinking wine straight from the bag and~~
~~repeating over and over again "You can either make love or die at the~~
~~hands of / the Cobra Commander". This is the tracing ribbon you cling~~
~~to. Something encoded in your mind provides a clue. You can cling to.~~
~~When you see a picture of your fifth grade classroom (yes, that's you in~~
~~the blue jumper, the plastic glasses so heavy you tipped your head, the~~
~~tinted acne cream that never matched your winter tan, all these as you~~
~~lean self-consciously into the pupil next to you in the hopes that you'll~~
~~remember wrong that that was a good year and you'll remember wrong~~
~~that you did get invited and she was loved her present) reminds you of~~
~~the way your mother smelled like salisbury steaks then. Remembering~~
~~wrong is still remembering.~~

A pulse is a crop full of seeds. A little vegetable bud. Not so big as a pea. At first a fruit, it becomes a vegetable when cooked. Mendel used them to create his theory of inheritance.

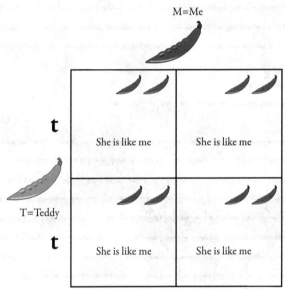

How Our Daughter Came to Be How She Is

When I first realized that she was not just an amalgamation of Teddy and me. In this way we had always hoped wouldn't happen: she is like me. This is how it began. With her pulse.

Where We Keep Who We Are

Teddy and I put another
pinwheel on Ben's grave

Facts about vegetables

My mother's favorite cashmere sweater

Shall I compare thee
to a plumber's weight

We'll put ranch dressing on anything

Use your long division you nincompoop

A terrible sunburn in Costa Rica

4,000 years ago the Chinese
invented noodles

My father had a brown mustache

Emily Dickinson's handwriting

Teddy's not terrified anymore. Jen and Gary offer to babysit while we go out for the first time in months. We didn't ask. They offered. In the car on the way to the bar we argue. We sit down to dinner and we argue:

[Look I'm important to her too. Quit taking her with you for entire days.]

{You're too loose in the world.}

[What the hell does that mean?]

{Hey, I heard onion rings are bad for short-term memory. Maybe you should lay off.}

[Fuck you.]

Afterwards we head to the bar to meet some of his work friends.
Teddy touches the arm of a woman he knows.
Unlike her I no longer have a piercing.
He loves that she's punctured.
I interrupt their conversation.

[I want to go home.]

I take the keys he leaves on the bar.
I want to tell him to remember when he was brave. But I walk out the
door.

At home, Jen and Gary don't know what to do and so they put their coats on when they see me walk in alone and leave without a word through the front door while I go to the room where she sleeps.

I look in on my daughter
turn my back on her
overwhelmed the way
the quilt wraps her
will never kiss her
scraped knees cannot kiss
what's not cut
can only tell her

[I'm sorry but this must be done.]

Rip this page.

Or I will.

Teddy brings her back to me. Before he's done walking through the door he says:

[Did you do anything stupid while I was gone?]

Instead of answering I pick her up and feel her forehead where the softspots have become not so. I don't watch Teddy watch me.

I don't watch Teddy watch me because I'm afraid of the look on his face. Because now he feels smart when he reminds me
{She is your daughter.}
Because now I feel relieved when I remember

[She is my daughter.]

Episodic memory: the day I brought my daughter home from the hospital I read to her from Ginsberg's "Kaddish" for a reason I can't recall but I do remember her eyes opening when I read "No more to say, and nothing to weep for but the Beings in the Dream, / trapped in its disappearance" and I remember Teddy said:

{For Christ's sake, at least read from Part 2. It's less depressing}

and being upset and I think this is when he started to write everything down. This is when it seemed he'd turned farther from me. Everything she does or when she blew a bubble or how her eyes move to follow me or how we wondered if her nervous system acts like an aspen grove or no matter how much we know that listening to classical music might help her spatially we can't resist the way she shakes her fists when we play Bob Dylan's "Lily, Rosemary, and the Jack of Hearts" and we wonder if it's the harmonica solo and hope she'll play it someday, or if she hears it too, the way Dylan smiles when he says the first "hearts" in the studio version, or whether somehow she knows that every time Teddy and I hear it we're back in that country, driving on the wrong side of the road, wondering whether we might demolish a cow with our car, smoking cigarettes and feeling like we would always be in the bunker of each other's heart. Or if she knows that I'm the only one clinging to.

I floss often now.

Frank Lloyd Wright. I see you.
Do not know why.
How am I going to keep you
Frank Lloyd Wright?

When someone first saw Fallingwater he said he looked at it and wanted to sing. I didn't know how that could be until her.

The architecture of my heart. She is. If we forget things so we can remember others, then let everything I've forgotten, everything I'm forgetting as you read this as I write it, keep her with me. I will not cling to the previous pages to see what I've since lost. I will keep the song I sing when I see her until the last moment.

Teddy has left me. She'll be in nursery school with everyone else next year. There was no reason to stay home. He still doesn't know. How we can be together in her. I get drunk in the afternoon and tell him when he's stopped by to pick up some pans:

[Who we are is the memory of who we are.]

This is what I wish for now. Neither of us knows what to do with that. I think he can almost understand what it might be like to be me. It's as if he believes he had no memory before her arrival. And because a belief is a memory it is so. He thinks he should be somewhere else with her. He says she will barely notice. I don't tell him what will happen when she loses a tooth. I want to hold it over his head. But if he knows, he will be worried. He'll let her become a petri dish before he lets her be with me. He believes they could live an uninterrupted existence separate from me. He believes that she should live with him. Will he remember threatening to expose me so I would let her leave with him? If at some point I forget him saying this. Does this make it not a fact?

When they are somewhere without me I remember when I got mad and slept with Teddy's friend John who did not know of my condition did not make me s~~hiver or feel regret for forgetting but did~~ cum.

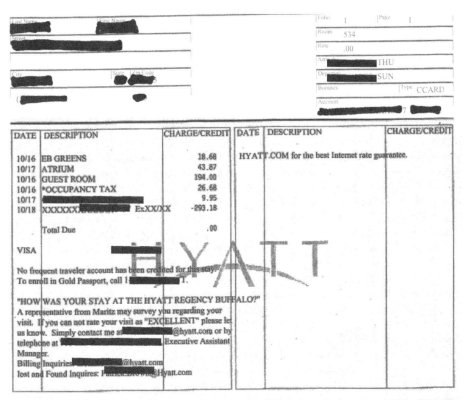

It is better if I forget.
I won't remember to feel guilty.
It is better if I forgot.

I should've
ripped this page.

That I cannot make a telephone ring.

That there's nothing left to feel guilty about ripping.

If memory defines us then where are we right now? If we are in memory, there could be Christmas music on as Teddy and I dance with one another in the kitchen. Someone wants to take a picture because we are so good together now. But we do not need a picture. Teddy's hands around my waist.

Knowing he was there then is not the same as having him here now. I want the him from then, now. I want the Teddy that is supposed to stay unchanged in my memory. And when we are doing our awkward steps, holding on, it's not useful to interrupt and say:

{We'll think of this when we're fifty.}

The places you go when you realize: I can't remember ever remembering this before.

She's getting bigger. I can brush her hair now. She says so many things more than her name. She's three and doesn't wear diapers. Now it's Jen who makes the phone ring, who doesn't stand outside the door but comes in. My daughter tells her she hasn't gone number two. When I ask her if she's tired she says:

{I am not tired. I am almost four.]

Sometimes she wants to sleep with a frisbee.

And she falls down often.
But we don't tell Teddy.

I remember that I have forgotten.
I poked my thumb on a staple in the upholstery.
If we cannot keep me from getting scratched, losing things, how will
we keep her.

I. How will
I keep her.

Please don't.
Rip this.

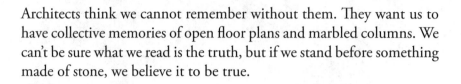

Architects think we cannot remember without them. They want us to have collective memories of open floor plans and marbled columns. We can't be sure what we read is the truth, but if we stand before something made of stone, we believe it to be true.

What then of something of paper?

Could this, what I've written, be a statue of myself.

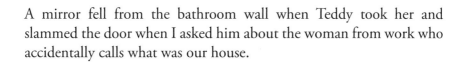

A mirror fell from the bathroom wall when Teddy took her and slammed the door when I asked him about the woman from work who accidentally calls what was our house.

He yelled:

{Why can't you forget to be jealous!}

and tells me he's taking our daughter to the park.

It's a reflex, to reach for the pieces of broken underneath.

I cut myself today. I remind myself. I am myself today. I cut myself. Today I remind myself I cut myself. I remind myself I am myself. Today I remind myself. I cut myself today.

I cut myself today. I remind myself. I am myself today. I cut myself. Today I remind myself I cut myself. I remind myself I am myself. Today I remind myself. I cut myself today.

You.
Ripped.
This page.

It is better.
I will keep her.
secrets he doesn't know what she won't remember.

She shouldn't always tell Teddy when she's bumped her head.

We are a kludge now. I think. On the first day of his new apartment when he picks her up for school and they go home and I live in this house. And I go through my things. And I wonder what he'll do when he finally knows.

Bees dance to make a map for others to know where the best nectar is. But hardly any bee pays attention. They don't want someone else's dance. They know the food is where they remember. It seems bees dance for no one.

The first afternoon home alone it comes to me. What I'm going to have to do.

I hope he will know when she needs reminding.

Narration is supposed to honor memory.
These pages need to be made of a kind of marble.
This is why I am writing this.
To nurse things from memory.

I wouldn't have done it if there hadn't been that
This is how it began.

Some doctors advise their patients to take the drug Propranolol. This is what it looks like:

For years people were administered this chemical for hypertension. But then they realized: Propranolol can remove emotional memory. If you take it, and you think about the car accident you were in last week, it stops your brain from sending stress hormones, stops the nerves from pulsating, stops the blood vessels from constriction. They say it doesn't take away the event: the car accident. Just the emotion attached to it.

This means that these parts are affected:

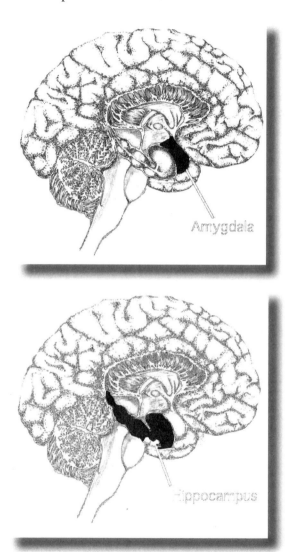

They are not affected. I will not unattach myself.

Do we have an obligation to remember? It is good for Teddy and me when I remember that day in the sand, or for my daughter, when I remember that first time she reached her hands towards me.

What about communal memory? You and I reading this.
As we write it.
Will we want to prevent the return of fear together? Should we take a drug so we don't hyperventilate when we get paper cuts?

It is good to remember?
Or it is a tragedy.

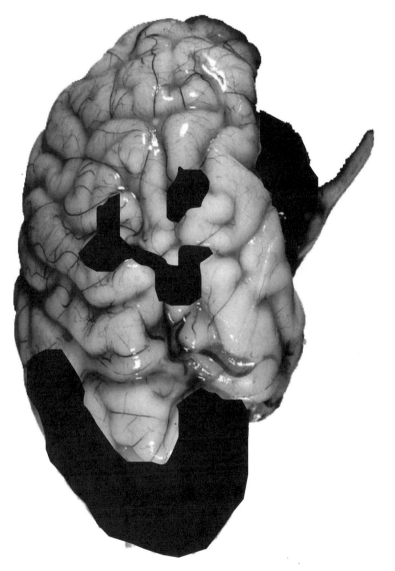

There are so many of these parts afflicted by memory.

I never wanted to be someone who clings to but I do cling to

The day it seemed like her eyes turned the color
they were always going to be.
Pumping her milk in that time of night
when there is no time
only the ticking of a thing above the stove.
Her pink umbrella.
The day she told her teacher that her parents weren't divorced
they just lived in different castles.

A reflex. How we define it now. An unlearned or involuntary response.

Or what a reflex used to be:

to be turned or cast back, as light
which means also to reflect.

Writing this is a reflex.
Like the way she reaches for me.
This is a reflex to reflect upon.

You and me. Reading this as it's written This reflex becomes a reflection.

An unlearned or involuntary response.
We take steps.
We speak.
We once reached for each other.
We see.

Can we forget something we never reflected on?

This began as I begin to understand why he used to make the telephone ring. When she comes home with a skinned knee will she remember which way the fishhook, the "J" in her name, should swing? When she asks us if she can pierce her ears Teddy tells her she's not old enough yet. I agree because I want to say to her:

[Don't you understand?
You just spent all of last week
learning the planets. They will keep you
company. Why would you want
to lose them?]

Around an absence. My identity tethered to a series of absences. Like how I can't remember how a new mother smells.

A map of my memory might look like

♃ Useless letters in Scrabble.

⊕ At 4,723 years old, Methuselah, the bristlecone pine, is the opposite of me.

♆ I cannot remember her name.

♂ It was squash salad.

⊕ Licking powdered sugar off our fingers on a bad day.

☿ Sober or not. He was mine.

☿ I cannot remember my name.

♄

I wouldn't have done it if there hadn't been that horsefly. This is how it begins.

Just because
you can't see it
doesn't mean
it's not ripped.

I wonder if I should go back to the beginning, write: "In Memory Of."
But what

She's almost six and has a tooth that's ready to come out. Teddy tells her the Tooth Fairy will come and even though we rarely speak these days we paint her a picture of wings made of cloud vapor and she's convinced the Fairy wears purple slippers that can become roller skates when she wants them to. Teddy tells me he will sneak underneath her pillow. Not because he's afraid of me bumping into something in the dark anymore. But because we are not a we. He never asks me anymore if anything has happened. He hasn't asked me about Indiana. Whether or not I can remember when he was in love with even my eyebrows. When he wrote them a love letter about the angles they sometimes made.

Teddy tells me he's with a different woman.
But our daughter will only ever call her Lesley. I tell him he'll bring her
back or I'll ~~fucking~~ ————————————————

He comes to the door.

I refuse him.
To cool to room temperature.
I refuse to let him.

I reach for his house keys with the Swiss Army Knife, pull up my shirt
to expose my ~~abdomen~~ ————

Make a contusion.

This is when he says

————————————————

This is when I knew I would do it.

There was the first contusion. When my hand trembled. There are more now. Writing through this rush of adrenaline to locate these memories that are prayers before what's needed to mend the ulnar artery leaves me. I think I remember that hands are rarely symmetrical anyway.
In unison with my heartbeat things run from me.

How to Baby Proof a House

Use a crib made after 1992.
Keep coins inside cupboards.
We should've covered the corners of the fireplace.
But we secured the bookshelves.

Some things leave me like no other memory.

I can make a telephone not ring.

A blow to the head. First ataxic aphasia[1]. The words are preserved but I can't find them with my tongue. My mouth won't form them. For the time being, I can still write through my deliberate infliction.

Signals near the railroad
ring each night
a train never comes
that I can hear
it is not that
I forget the train
it is
not that I forgot?

1. Even if I could I wouldn't say that I want to be underneath his fingernails again.

This page I will rip.
And every page after.
What's begun is passed
Too fast for you to keep up.
The pages I've ripped out
would only slow this down.

i dream of
streams of gauze well placed
cuts so the treetop will fall
long enough of them
even functions incapable
of being forgotten
get forgotten

I saw into bone as ~~best I can James Tate's~~ "Fuck the
~~Astronauts" comes to me and his~~ "~~memory's~~ dark ink in your
last smile" ~~as I~~

   my last hand trembles.
          the harmonica solo

                      ——— static to clot

when we forget ~~sentences we~~ write poetry

there was dark blue before there was blue.

Memory is not a
sense it is the
principal capacity
of the soul

My daughter
let her close this
with these words
to become a moment later
perfectly innocent of its contents

let it giver her a paper cut

SHORT FLIGHT / LONG DRIVE BOOKS
a division of HOBART
PO Box 1658
Ann Arbor, MI 48106
www.hobartpulp.com/minibooks

ISBN: 978-0-9825301-6-0

Printed in the United States of America
First Edition

Inside text set in Garamond

This book exists because of everything Beth Nugent ever did and the city of Chicago and Louie Holwerk (the breakfast hound) and Loulipo and the constraint A D Jameson came up with in 2006 and Greg the bartender at Jackie's where much of this was written and Adam Janusz who showed me how to open InDesign and Laird Hunt and Brian Kiteley and Shawn Huelle, whose name should be here twice for all the times he so generously read every draft and Aaron Burch and Elizabeth Ellen and my parents, Bill and Melodie Wigent and Richard Prouty, my grandfather, to whom some parts of this book are dedicated and of course and always and most, my husband, Frank.